A
FISHY TAIL

To: Pinnie

with best wishes

Barbara Spencer

BARBARA SPENCER

Illustrated by Charley Belles

Matador
9 Priory Business Park
Kibworth Beauchamp
Leicestershire LE8 0RX, UK
Tel: (+44) 116 279 2299
Fax: (+44) 116 279 2277
Email: books@troubador.co.uk
Web: www.troubador.co.uk/matador

ISBN 9781780882444

British Library Cataloguing in Publication Data.
A catalogue record for this book is available from the British Library.

Illustrations and cover: Charley Belles
Chapter headings: Aimee Hibberd
Designed by Lorraine Inglis
Typeset in Novaresse Book

Printed and bound in the UK by TJ International, Padstow, Cornwall

Matador is an imprint of Troubador Publishing Ltd

To: Kairi and Theo
'who swim like little fishes'

Other books by Barbara Spencer

For Children
Scruffy
A Dangerous Game of Football
The Bird Children

For Young Adults
Running
Time Breaking

2012
Legend of the Five Javean

A
FISHY TAIL

BARBARA SPENCER

My family

Beastly Glasses

'I hate it, I won't eat it, I won't,' shouted Micky, staring down at his plate.

'Oh dear,' said his mother, 'but you liked it last week, it was your favourite.'

'I don't like it this week.'

'Oh dear,' said Mrs Wells, sounding very anxious now because she couldn't find anything that Micky liked to eat. He loathed spinach and peas, beans and carrots, cabbage and eggs, and sausages and fish, AND being the youngest.

'Why can't I be old like David and Penny? It's no fun being the youngest,' he stormed. 'They hate me and they never let me do things with them.'

'Oh, I'm sure they don't hate you, Micky.'

'Yes, they do,' he grumbled. 'David calls me a disgrace to mankind – and I don't even know what that is – and Penny says I should carry a health warning.

'It's so unfair. Why can't David have a go at being the youngest – why has it always got to be me? I was the youngest at five AND six AND seven AND I'm the littlest. They're always telling me I'm too little to do things. Why am I so little, Mum?'

'Because you're the youngest, Micky,' said Mrs Wells – a little unwisely.

'But I HATE being the youngest. It's beastly having to go to bed first and miss all the good stuff on telly.'

'Oh *dear*,' said Mrs Wells sounding very upset indeed.

Micky stomped upstairs to his room and flung himself on the bed. He glared at his reflection in the mirror, a mop of black hair with his face all blurred and fuzzy round the edges. Angrily, he hooked his thumbs into the corners of his mouth, pulled down his eyelids, crossed his eyes and stuck out his tongue. The face glaring back at him looked disgusting, but it was still blurred and fuzzy at the edges.

'Don't put up with it,' said Mr Wells that evening after Micky had finally gone to bed.

'And what do you suggest I do?'

'Send him to his room without any supper.'

'He'll be thrilled,' said Mrs Wells, 'he hates eating.'

'So why not ask the twins to talk to him,' suggested Mr Wells.

'I've tried. David just calls Micky a miserable little worm.'

'And Penny? Surely she's more sensible.'

'Oh no, she's no better,' sighed Mrs Wells. 'She can't bear Micky anywhere near her in case he gets his dirty hands on her clean dress. It's very difficult being seven, you know.'

'Nonsense!' Mr Wells sounded irritated. 'It's no more difficult being seven than … er … forty-seven.' (Mr Wells was forty-seven) 'Anyway Micky's nearly eight!'

'It's just the same at seven or eight,' snapped Mrs Wells. 'You've stopped being a baby, but everyone still treats you like one. Please do something. I can't bear having difficult children.'

'All right, my dear,' Mr Wells patted his wife's hand. 'Now, don't you worry, I'll think of something.'

But Mr Wells didn't think of anything straight away and meanwhile Micky continued to hate everything except hamburgers and ice cream, and everyone except his dad and mum. He even told his mum he hated her (he didn't really), because he had to go to the dentist for a check-up and to the opticians to have his eyes tested.

'I won't wear glasses,' he stormed. 'It's *so unfair*. David and Penny don't wear glasses.'

'I know, dear, and I'm so sorry. But if you wear them now, the doctor says by the time you're twelve – like David and Penny – your eyes will be stronger and then, hopefully, you can leave them off.'

'But twelve's years away,' protested Micky weeping. 'I'm not even eight yet, then there's nine and ten AND eleven. I shall be an old man before I'm twelve.'

'Dearest Micky,' his mum hugged him. 'I promise you won't be an old man at twelve. But do wear your glasses, just to please me.'

'Can I have hamburgers for tea?'

Mrs Wells gave in. 'Yes, you can have hamburgers if you wear your glasses.'

But in one week Micky had succeeded in breaking them; and in one month he was on his fourth pair.

'Now I've had quite enough of this,' said his dad crossly. 'If you lose or break this pair, I shall stop your pocket money and you will NOT watch television until you learn to behave.'

So Micky wore his glasses and added his dad to his list of hates.

Then Mr Wells *did* think of something.

'I have news!' he bellowed as he opened the front door. 'And it's great news. David! Penny! Micky! Come here!'

Micky dropped his book on the floor and tore downstairs, closely followed by the twins.

'*De-Dar*,' Mr Wells shouted, beating a drum-roll on an imaginary drum. 'You'll never guess in a million years!'

'WHAT?' shouted Micky.

'WE – ARE – GOING – TO – LIVE – IN – BARBADOS – FOR – A – WHOLE – YEAR.'

'WHERE?' said David and Penny, speaking together.

'WHEN?' said his wife.

'WHAT'S BARBADOS?' said Micky.

'It's an island in the Caribbean Sea, a long way from here. The sun shines every day, not like here where it's cold and miserable half the time. I have to go there for work and we leave in four weeks – just after Micky's birthday. Get the map, Micky.'

The vast outline of the coast of America appeared. Tucked away in a semi-circle of dots, Micky saw a small, green oblong surrounded by a sea of blue. David and Penny chased off to search the encyclopaedia for information, leaving their dad, with Micky perched on his knee, to point out the plane route from England.

'And can I learn to swim?' Micky said, when he heard about the blue water of the Caribbean Sea and all the sailing boats.

'But you hate swimming,' interrupted Mrs Wells.

'Not in Barbados, I don't. I just love swimming in Barbados,' said Micky triumphantly out-manoeuvring his mother.

Micky was so excited he actually forgot to make a fuss about having to go to bed first.

'I can't wait,' he cried. 'A month is ages and ages and ages. Why it's four weeks, which is … er …'

'Ages!' Mum laughed. 'It's all right for you, you've only got to pack your suitcase, I have the whole house to pack; I'll never be ready in a month.'

"And can I learn to swim?" Micky said.

Islands in the Sun

The great day arrived. Micky was so excited he could hardly eat his breakfast. He watched for the taxi to take them to Heathrow Airport, his nose pressed against the windowpane. And he asked, at least a hundred times, 'Mum, when's the taxi going to arrive?'

At last, with a screeching of brakes and a loud blast from its horn, the taxi pulled up at the front door. Next minute, the family were off. Micky stared out of the taxi window, his nose pressed against the glass, watching to see his first airplane. And he asked, at least a hundred times, 'Mum, will we be there soon.'

'Look a plane,' he shouted suddenly, making them all jump. 'There it is, see!' Micky held his breath as the monster climbed into the sky, trailing exhaust fumes behind it.

The airport would have been exciting even if Micky hadn't been catching a plane, with people there from every country in the world, many of them wearing clothes quite different from Micky's jeans and jacket. He kept asking David, 'Where does that man come from?' and 'Where's that?' because most of the countries he'd never heard of: Kenya, Nigeria and Sudan.

They checked their luggage and, once their flight had been called, walked down, what seemed like, a million identical corridors – all with moving-walkways. They walked so far that Micky began to wonder if they were walking to Barbados.

'It's huge,' Micky whispered to his brother as they finally boarded their plane. 'It's bigger than our house.'

Actually, the plane was bigger than four houses. And, by the time Micky had explored, watched the stewards serve everyone a drink, it was time for lunch. He ate every bit, it was so delicious.

'Micky you've eaten your carrots?' His mother pointed at his clean plate. 'But you never eat carrots,' she continued amazed. 'You don't like carrots.'

'Oh, I like carrots now,' he said. 'I just didn't like English carrots.'

Mrs Wells was speechless. She glanced at her husband who grinned happily at her and carried on eating.

'Told you so,' he whispered between mouthfuls.

The journey was really long and took nearly nine hours. David, Penny, and Micky played cards, read, watched the movie, slept a little, and listened to their radios. Gradually it got warmer and, just as Micky was beginning to think they never would arrive, the Seat Belt sign flashed on. The plane began to descend; hardly noticeable at first until Micky felt his ears go *pop*. Then, with a series of horrendous groans and thumps, the wheels dropped into place. The plane banked tilting sideways and, through the small porthole window, Micky caught sight of the sea. He couldn't believe his eyes. It was blue exactly like the pictures his dad had shown him, deep, deep blue. And he could see straight down to the bottom.

'Can I go in the sea straight away?' he shouted, trying to bounce up and down in his seat with his seat belt fastened. 'It looks smashing, ever so friendly, not like the sea in England which looks cross.'

'Micky, you are just like the sea,' his mother laughed at him. 'You're always cross in England, too.'

'Can I, Dad?' he said. 'Can I go in the sea straight away?'

'Not today, Micky. You've got a whole year and the sea will be there tomorrow, just as friendly.'

The big jet touched down onto the tarmac, its engines screeching loudly as it slowed down. It taxied across the runway, following a truck on which were painted the words, Follow Me. They arrived at their parking bay and the engines died away.

By the time the crew had opened the doors, most of the passengers were already out of their seats, blocking up the aisle. Out of the plane they rushed into a burst of warm, sunny wind. Down the steep flight of steps, across the tarmac, with its black and white zebra crossing, and into the terminal. No moving pavements, only trees and flowers and the bright colours of sunshine.

'It's not like England, is it?' Micky whispered to Penny who was walking beside him.

'No,' she whispered back. 'But it feels very comfy not strange at all.'

'Wow!' he exclaimed. 'That's exactly how I feel.'

The Arrivals Hall was hot and sunny with lots of people and lots of queues. Finally, it was Micky's turn to cross the big red line in front of the Immigration desk. He handed his passport to the officer.

'How long are you staying?' The tall man in a white uniform peered down at him.

'A whole year,' Micky boasted. 'My dad's come to work here. Is a year a long time?' he asked as the officer handed him back his passport.

'Yes, sir. A *whole* long time. Long enough to get a nice tan and take plenty of sea baths.'

They smiled at one another, and Micky moved on.

'I like Barbados,' he announced as they waited for their luggage. 'I'm going to like it very much indeed.'

# Moving

 House

And he did like it. The sun shone every day from six in the morning till six at night. It was warm and happy, not cold and rainy; although almost everything was different. There were no postmen or milkmen. You had to fetch your letters from the post office and only the big supermarket sold fresh milk. Instead, people used powdered or tinned. And some of the buses were so old and battered, they had blinds instead of glass for windows.

When Mum told Micky they had to stay in a hotel until their baggage arrived by boat, he didn't believe her. Every day he asked when the furniture lorry was going to bring his books and games. Finally, Dad decided to take Micky to the port to see the ships dock.

'You see, Micky,' he explained as they watched the men unloading wood from a cargo boat, 'this is a very small island. Instead of using lorries to carry goods from town to town, the people here use boats to deliver goods from island to island.'

On the day the boat carrying their baggage was expected, they went down to the harbour to watch it dock;

dozens of men running around with ropes and chains to secure the ship. Then Micky really did believe in a furniture van which sailed on water. But he still couldn't get his toys.

'They start unloading tonight and Customs will clear them tomorrow, so let's go early.'

They set off at seven with Mr Wells clutching a large bundle of papers. First, they went to one office to get some papers signed, then they went to another office where more papers were signed; and there were so many papers and so many offices that it took all day! But, finally, everything was sorted.

'I saw green bananas being put on a huge boat,' Micky told his mother that evening. 'It's called a Geest Boat and it comes here every Tuesday. And everyone was very kind, they gave me a Coke and a fish sandwich for lunch – it was great.'

Mrs Wells stared at Micky in astonishment. 'But you hate fish, Micky.'

'Do I?' said Micky. 'Don't think so, Mum. You've got me mixed up with David.'

There's no doubt about it, thought Micky. *This is a great place. Everything's great – school's great – the food's great – and the beach is really great – and soon I'll be able to swim.* School was a terrific adventure too, except that he didn't much like the cane the teacher carried.

'In England,' he boasted proudly to his new friends, 'you can only get detentions and you have to do something really *bad* first.'

'And you're still too little!'

But after three months the sun was still shining, the people were still friendly, school was okay, the beach was still there – and he still couldn't swim. Bored and miserable, Micky mooched around the house.

'Why can't I come to the beach with you and Penny?' he asked David, as soon as he got in from school. 'I promise I won't be a nuisance.'

'Because you're too little.'

'That's not fair. You said I was too little when I was seven. I'm eight now.'

'And, you're still too little.' David stuck his tongue out. 'Come on, Penny, let's go before the nuisance breaks into tears.'

'Mu-um will you take me? I've nothing to do.'

'Sorry, Micky, I'm just too busy today, we'll go on Saturday.'

'I hate being eight; it's just like being seven. I'm still too little to do things. I hate Barbados. I want to go home to England,' he grumbled.

'Oh, Micky, not again,' his mother groaned. 'I can't bear it. If you've said that once, you've said it fifty times. For *goodness sake* go away and play.' Mrs Wells didn't mean to speak so sharply.

Micky stormed out of the house slamming the door behind him. He plunged into a chair on the veranda, staring moodily at the garden, and kicked his feet in the dust. It wasn't fair always being the youngest. No one loved him and he had nothing to do in this mouldy old place.

Gran + Grandad they'd be
pleased to sea him all right

Then he had a most brilliant idea. He'd go back to England. The more he thought about it, the more brilliant it became. All his friends were there *and* Gran and Granddad. They'd be pleased to see him all right AND they let him do stuff AND they never *got cross* with him AND they didn't nag.

But where could he find a boat? Micky frowned. Bridgetown harbour had lots of boats but if he went there he might bump into his dad, or one of his Dad's friends, and THEY would want to know what he was doing on his own. Suddenly, he remembered the small fishing town they had passed as they drove in from the airport. He'd seen lots of boats there.

'I bet one of them will take me to England,' he muttered. *So that was that.* He'd go.

Micky stuck his head through the kitchen door. His mother was busy cooking and didn't look round.

'What do you want now, Micky?'

'I don't want any dinner,' he announced. 'I'm going back to England, *so there.*'

'Yes, do that, dear,' said Mum, not listening to a word he said.

Micky slammed the door shut. *That's that then*, he thought. And set off for the bus stop.

unning way

Several buses passed without stopping, filled to the brim with laughing school children. Finally, one did stop and he got on, everyone squashing up a bit to make room.

The road was narrow and the bus stopped frequently to let passengers off. Behind it a little queue of cars had gathered, waiting patiently for it to set off again. It growled its way up slopes between banks of sand and scrub, where mango and casuarina trees, with prickly green fronds, grew wild; and brown sheep, that looked more like goats, grazed. It passed houses with balconies and scarlet poinsettias growing in the garden; and bungalows, painted blue or green, with red galvanised-iron roofs. It swerved round little lines of people walking along the road; the women carrying babies and using umbrellas to shield them from the sun.

Micky peered under a lady's elbow to see out of the window, trying to remember exactly where the town was. *There!* He recognised it now. Reaching across, he rang the bell. The bus screeched to a halt and he leapt off onto the dusty road.

The town appeared to be quite small, only a main street

with houses set out all higgledy-piggledy, not in rows like in England. Some of these were really old too, like little wooden boxes on stilts, with geraniums and straggly pot plants growing in rusty tins on the front steps. On the far side of the road was the seashore, with its fishing boats arranged in neat rows along a white sandy beach.

The bus had stopped by an old rum shop. Through its open wooden doors, Micky saw a group of fishermen talking and laughing together as they drank their rum, while the radio chattered away in the background. Micky walked slowly across the road towards the boats. Opposite him, on the edge of the sand, was a big stone table. Earlier that morning, it had been surrounded by a crowd of gossiping women, eager to buy fresh fish from the boats as they came in from the sea. Now it was deserted, except for the town dogs fighting for the bits of fish that had dropped on to the ground. Micky wrinkled up his nose. *Pooh, it did smell.*

Nearby, tucked into the shade of a fishing boat, a little group of fishermen were mending a large hole in one of their nets. They seemed friendly, joking among themselves as they worked.

'Excuse me, sirs,' Micky asked in his politest voice.

The men looked up.

'Could you please tell me where I can hire a boat to go to England?'

They stared at him in silence for a moment. Then, one of them spoke.

'An what you wantgo England for?'

Now Micky couldn't give an honest answer. He couldn't say he hated Barbados because that would be rude. Instead he said, 'My home's in England and I feel homesick.'

'Hmm!' The man chewed on his pipe thoughtfully, inspecting Micky closely. 'Where your parents, they in England?' he said at last.

'No!' Micky shook his head. 'They're here but they don't care much about me, so I'm going back to England. I can pay, look.' He pulled a crumpled five-dollar bill from his pocket, which was his pocket money for the week.

'Boy, you talkin' nonsense, we don't go to England,' burst out the youngest man in the group.

'Hush up!' warned the older man. 'Son, you go and ask dat old man on de beach here.' He pointed to the far end of the beach. 'He take boys to England all de time.'

Micky thanked him and swung round to look. At the far end of the white sandy beach, he could just make out a figure sitting in the shade of a fishing boat.

'Why you tell him dat?' said the young fisherman angrily. 'Why you not give him some good lashes in his tail and send him home?'

'Boy,' said the older man sternly. 'You've got a lot to learn. If dat poor chile wants to run away, it far better he go with old Grandpa. He'll take good care of him.'

He grinned round at his friends. They nodded, turning to watch the boy as he made his way along the sand.

Micky stopped a little way away from the brightly coloured boat, peering at it closely. It was larger than the other boats on the beach, with newly painted stripes of green and turquoise. Now he could see the figure more clearly, it was an old man with a long white beard. He was sitting quite still, gazing out to sea and, perched on the rail above him, was a large white pelican, its head tucked under its wing.

He's *awfully old*, Micky thought, gazing at the white beard. I *wonder if he's too old to go to England. Well, he could only ask.*

The old man was wearing a shawl round his shoulders. Micky thought this was most peculiar, because it was scorching hot, even the old man was sitting in the shade. But still more peculiar, the shawl appeared to be made of seaweed.

Micky coughed. 'Excuse me. I'm looking for a boat to go to England.'

The old man got to his feet in one swift movement.

'I'm just about to set out for England,' he said. He had sparkling brown eyes that seemed to look right through Micky. 'The fare is five dollars if you're interested.'

'Oh yes, please.' Micky pulled out his note and handed it over. 'When do we go?'

'Now, as soon as you're aboard. Have you got your passport?'

Micky's hand flew to his mouth. *Oh dear, he'd forgotten all about passports.*

'Never mind,' the old man didn't wait for Micky's reply. 'You'll just have to stay below till we clear the island. Hop aboard.'

'Is it far to England?'
he asked dejectedly

So Micky hopped aboard and so did the pelican, who perched on the cabin top. The old man climbed in and the boat slid quietly into the water.

Micky stared. *There wasn't anyone in sight to push it into the water, so how …*

'It's automatic,' said the old man reading Micky's thoughts. 'Now, lad, you'd better go below, there's plenty there to interest you.' He pointed towards the closed doors of the wheelhouse. Micky crossed the deck and, pulling open the doors, peered in. He gave a gasp of astonishment and tumbled eagerly down the steps into the cabin.

A Boat to England

The cabin wasn't a bit like a real fishing boat, with bunks and nets and fishing tackle: it was more like an underwater cave and shone with a greenish light. Micky searched for a light switch but couldn't find one. Then he wondered if the weird colour came from the green seaweed which draped the cabin from floor to ceiling. The floor was covered with a thick carpet of sand and, scattered on top, were seashells: white shells and pink shells – which looked like butterfly wings, conch shells, sea dollars, and oyster shells. He stared about him, his mouth gaping open like a fish.

There were fish, too. As his eyes adjusted to the strange glow, Micky could see them quite clearly. He picked up a frond of seaweed and peered more closely, watching them weave their way in and out of the strands – exactly as if they were swimming.

They can't be real fish, he thought, *they have to be stuffed.*

Micky was so absorbed in his discovery that, at first, he hardly noticed the boat moving. Then the fish began to bob up and down, instead of swaying gracefully, and the

Watching them weave their way in and out of the strands — exactly as if they were swimming.

boat began to dance a jig. Next moment, it was rocking violently from side to side and from bow to stern as it met the oncoming waves.

Micky began to feel very peculiar as if he were bobbing up and down, like the fish. His head whirled round and round, like the spin-cycle on his mother's washing machine, while his tummy felt as if it was about to explode.

'Oh dear,' he groaned. He sat down on the steps and held his head. The swaying of the boat was worse and so was he. He rushed up the steps and, pulling open the cabin door, dashed on to the deck and over to the side rail, where he was violently sick.

The old man steering the boat appeared to notice nothing unusual. Humming a tune, he gazed steadily into the distance but the pelican turned to watch Micky, his head still over the rail.

After a bit Micky, still looking rather pale, sat down by the rail. 'Is it far to England?' he asked dejectedly.

'Oh, yes, quite some ways yet,' the old man replied.

'And will the sea stay rough?'

'Bound to, we're heading for the Atlantic Ocean.'

Micky groaned. He remembered his father showing him the Atlantic Ocean on the map. Then he remembered that the plane journey had taken nine hours.

'Will your boat take as long as the plane?' he said in a timid whisper.

'About the same, I guess,' said the boatman and the pelican squawked in agreement.

'And how long have we gone so far?' said Micky, after he'd been sick a second time.

'Mm, quite a long way, give or take a little,' said the old man, still humming cheerfully.

Micky groaned again. He *must already have been at least two hours on the boat*. He quickly counted: *three, four, five – seven more hours!*

'Please, sir, do you think we could go back to Barbados? You see,' he tried to explain, the words tumbling over one another. 'I didn't think it would take so long and I don't really want my parents to worry about me.'

'But I thought you said they didn't care about you.'

'Oh no, they love me very much,' Micky said in a rush and stopped. *He hadn't told the old man anything about his parents.*

'But what about England? Don't you want to go any more?' asked the old fisherman. 'We could set out again in the morning, if you wished.'

'Oh no,' Micky hastily replied. 'I really have to go home now and anyway, I don't think I want to go back to England without my family, thank you all the same.'

'Well, that's fine then,' said the old man heartily, turning the boat around. And the pelican, shuffling along the rail, rubbed its beak along the boy's arm in a friendly way.

Immediately, (or was it only Micky's imagination) the boat stopped rocking and he stopped feeling sick. In fact, he began to enjoy the ride, the boat skimming over the little white waves. All too soon he could see the island with its King Palm trees on the hills; then people on the shore. And, in a twinkling, the boat was running up on to the beach.

'Gosh, that was quick,' exclaimed Micky.

'Well, it doesn't take long, once you decide to go home.'

Micky gulped. 'Oh, whatever will I say to my mum? I have to be home by five and I must be awfully late. She'll be ever so cross.'

'No need to worry,' said the old man, in his comfortable manner. 'That's all taken care of and you'll be home before your mother even notices you've gone.'

Micky sat silent for a few minutes and then burst out. 'I didn't really mean to run away but ...' he stopped.

'But what?'

Suddenly Micky wanted to tell him. Without knowing why he felt sure the old man would understand.

'Sometimes, everything is hateful.' He stopped, not knowing how to go on.

'I remember being eight years old,' said the old man.

'You were eight years old!' exclaimed Micky interrupting him.

'Well, it was a very long time ago.' The old man smiled. 'What I'm trying to tell you is that everyone was eight once in their lives, even your parents. The trouble with people is they forget what it's like to be young. Now, take your brother, David. He's only twelve and he's forgotten already, just as if he'd never been eight at all. That's why he gets impatient with you. What you really need is to do one thing well. Then it won't matter about being the youngest and having to go to bed early and wear glasses.'

Micky stared, completely tongue-tied, his mouth once again gaping open like a fish.

'Surprised you, have I? Thought I was too old with my long, white beard to take a boat to England?'

The old man chuckled and the pelican opened its beak and flapped its wings, as if it too were laughing.

Micky grinned back a bit shamefaced. 'How do you know all that?' he said. 'Are you a wizard?'

'Well, something of the sort.'

'Is that why you wear a seaweed shawl?'

'Good-gracious me, no! That's to keep me warm. Now don't you concern yourself about how I know things. Let's solve your problem. What do you want to do most?'

'Swim, of course,' Micky said, without hesitation.

'What, you can't swim! Well, that's easily fixed. Come and see me tomorrow and I'll teach you.'

'You will, *you really will*. Oh, that's terrific. What time tomorrow?'

'Now, let me see,' pondered the old man, scratching his beard. 'Is it Saturday tomorrow?'

Micky nodded his head furiously.

'Well, then, any time. I'll be here when you arrive. By the way,' he added handing Micky his five-dollar bill. 'You'd better have your fare back as we didn't go to England.'

'Oh no, sir.' Micky eyed the note, all the money he had for the week. 'It was my fault we didn't go. I can't possibly take it, that wouldn't be fair.'

'Suppose I take one dollar, to cover the distance we travelled, and return you four dollars. That's about right.' The old man appeared to be speaking to the pelican. It nodded its head and squawked. 'Now off you go home and by this tomorrow, I'll have you swimming like a fish.'

'Oh! Thank you, thank you. Goodbye.' Micky turned and vaulted over the side of the boat onto the sand. He started to run up the beach towards the bus stop, turning round to wave as he ran.

He passed the group of fishermen. The one that had spoken to him before, called out, 'Aren't you agoin to England, then?'

'No,' shouted Micky, 'I'm going to learn to swim instead.'

The fisherman took his pipe out of his mouth and pointed in the direction of the boy.

'Well, you see'd what I tells you. Old Grandpa, he gone done it again. Dat's one satisfied customer. Next time, lad, you remember, you send 'em down to see old Grandpa.' Putting his pipe back in his mouth, he chuckled cheerfully and went back to work.

A Puzzling Puzzle

Micky was exceptionally quiet that evening. In fact he hardly spoke at all, he was so busy thinking. He ate his dinner, without even looking to see what it was, and didn't even notice when his mother gave him chocolate ice cream – his favourite.

You see, if Micky had been younger he might have accepted all the strange things which had happened. After all, at seven you can still believe in wizards; but at eight – definitely not.

He sat in his chair, chin in his hands, going over and over what had happened and he couldn't explain any of it. But the most puzzling thing of all, when he arrived back home, the clock said five minutes to five. His mum was just beginning to prepare dinner and hadn't even noticed Micky had been out.

Micky heaved a sigh. *He would have to ask the old man tomorrow. But perhaps there wasn't an old man? Perhaps he'd imagined that too? Oh no! Then he wouldn't be able to learn how to swim.*

He jumped hastily to his feet. 'Mum, can I go to bed?'

There was a stunned silence. Everyone stopped what he

was doing to stare at Micky. He blushed and looked at the floor.

'Micky, what *is* going on?' demanded his dad. 'You have *never* in your life asked to go to bed.'

'Well … um … you see …' Micky shuffled his feet. 'I … er … met this old fisherman today. He said I could go for a ride on his boat tomorrow and he'd teach me to swim. He keeps his boat at that fishing town near the airport.' Micky mumbled the last bit, hoping his dad wouldn't ask what he was doing so far from home. 'And I thought if I went to bed early, tomorrow will come quicker.'

'Oh, is that all,' said his dad, looking relieved. He knew that in Barbados it was quite safe for children to go for a ride in a fishing boat.

'I think perhaps I'd better come with you,' said his mum, 'and meet this fisherman. What time did he say?'

'Oh any time,' replied Micky eagerly. 'But can we go early so I can learn to swim quicker?'

Mum laughed. 'We'll go for nine o'clock. Will that suit?'

'That's fantastic.'

'Now, for goodness sake, Micky, settle down and read a book,' ordered his dad. 'Tomorrow will come soon enough.'

But tomorrow didn't come soon enough. That night was a really long one. It took ages for Micky to fall asleep. When at last he did, he dreamed about swimming the English Channel all the way to France.

He got up early and by seven o'clock was ready to leave. He wandered about, in and out of the door, watching the clock. Finally, Mrs Wells threatened not to let him go at all, if he didn't sit quietly until she had finished her jobs. At last, she went to fetch her bag and car keys.

'Are you ready?' she called.

But Micky was already sitting in the car, his swimming shorts and towel under his arm. He didn't know quite how he felt. His stomach was hurtling round and round like a concrete mixer. He was excited, but also scared and anxious in case the old man had forgotten about him and wasn't there. He sat quietly in the car, with his fingers crossed tightly, giving a tremendous shout of, 'There he is', when he spotted the old man waiting for them by the side of the road.

'Good morning, Mrs Wells,' greeted the fisherman. 'I'm so glad you decided to bring Micky this morning so I can meet you.'

'I'm sorry,' said Mrs Wells as she shook hands with him, 'Micky hasn't told me your name.'

'The fishermen call me Old Grandpa, but my real name is Horatio Brown.'

'Well, Mr Brown, I am delighted to meet you. Thank you so much for offering to teach Micky to swim. Are you sure he won't be a nuisance?'

'Of course not, madam. I teach children to swim all the time. He will be quite safe with me and I will see he is home well in time for his dinner.'

The old man had such a comfortable air about him that Mrs Wells felt quite happy leaving Micky, so she said goodbye and drove off.

Mr Brown and Micky crossed the road and set off towards the far corner of the beach, Micky skipping happily at Mr Brown's side.

'Mr Brown, sir ...' Micky started to speak, then hesitated. 'You really are a wizard, aren't you?' he said finally.

The old man looked down at him. 'Oh, you mean the business of the time,' he said, once again reading Micky's thoughts. 'That's simple. Time passes slowly on my boat. You thought you'd been on it for hours and hours but it was only about fifteen minutes. Because you felt seasick, it seemed much longer – simple really.'

'Oh!' said Micky, still not convinced. 'Hey,' he shouted as they reached the boat. 'Your pelican's brought along a friend.'

There, perched on the stern rail, were two birds.

'This is Hector,' said the old man, pointing to the pelican.

'And this is his good friend, Lysander. He, by the way, is a cormorant.'

The two birds nodded their heads in greeting and Hector, who was somewhat the bigger of the two, winked at Micky, who winked back.

The boat moved down the beach and into the sea on its own, exactly as it had done the day before. Mr Brown stood by the wheel, whistling cheerily, while the two birds perched on the rail with Micky sitting beside them.

'Where are we going?' he said.

'To a reef close by, where I have lots of friends. There you can learn to swim safely, because the water is always calm and clear.'

'Will I have arm bands to keep me afloat?'

'Good gracious!' the old man exclaimed, sounding startled. 'Arm bands indeed. All you need are those.' He nodded in the direction of the cabin.

By the cabin door lay a pair of green fins. At least, when Micky first looked at them they were green.

Next minute they were deep blue.

No, they were green!

He gazed suspiciously at the old man as he steered the boat towards a patch of clear green sea; so clear you could see down to the sand beneath. There was something rather extraordinary about this particular wizard. (Micky was absolutely positive Mr Brown was a wizard, whatever he said to the contrary.)

'Right, here we are.'

The boat slowed to a stop as Mr Brown switched off the engine and threw the anchor overboard. It lay quietly, lifting a little as the waves rocked it.

'Now, young Micky, put on the fins.'

Micky did as he was told. His feet felt extraordinarily clumsy, nearly falling as he tried to walk.

'Over the side with you,' said Mr Brown, calmly seating himself on the side of the boat.

'But I *can't swim*, I'll drown!' protested Micky.

'Drown? You can't drown with those fins on. Whoever heard of such a thing,' he joked, and the birds flapped their wings in amusement.

'Very well, watch Lysander. He'll show you what to do. He may be a bird but he swims very well. Off you go, Lysander.'

Lysander dived straight into the water, his black neck outstretched, his wings folded close by his side. Micky could see him moving fast. He emerged with a flapping fish in his beak and, climbing back on board again, calmly swallowed it – tail, head, fins and all.

'Do you think you can do that?' said Mr Brown.

Micky swallowed nervously, hoping Mr Brown didn't mean the bit about catching and eating a fish.

'I think so,' he said timidly. 'I'll try anyway.'

Removing his glasses first, he climbed awkwardly on to the rail. He hesitated staring down at the green sea. Then, taking a quick breath, jumped in.

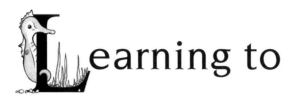earning to wim

The green water closed over Micky's head and he found
himself swimming just under the surface.

'I can swim,' he shouted. 'It's easy.'

'Well, I told you it was.'

The old man's voice seemed to come from just behind
him. Micky swung round to see where his friend was and
came face to face with a huge fish.

'HELP! Mr Brown, help! Quickly! It's a shark!'

In panic, Micky tried to swim out of the path of the fish.

'Calm down, boy, it's me,' laughed the old man's voice.
Micky shook his head trying to clear it. The voice came
from the fish. 'I'm no shark. I'm still Mr Brown.'

Micky couldn't believe his ears. The fish was talking to him.

'B-b-but you're a fish,' he exclaimed.

'A kingfish actually. So are you – except you are a lot
smaller than me. Well, you did ask if I was a wizard, didn't
you?' The huge fish was shaking
with laughter. 'Do you realise, Micky,
you're swimming upside down?'

Micky looked. Through the green water he could see the surface of the sea and the shape of the boat.

'Oh, so I am. What do I do now?' he said.

'Pull the water back with your left arm and point your head downwards.'

Micky did as he was told and found himself facing the reef again.

'That's right. Now use your feet to carry you along and keep your arms by your sides.'

Micky tried kicking his feet and found himself swimming on his side, facing the kingfish.

'Oh dear,' he sighed, 'I do feel funny. What's happening?'

'You're using one foot more than the other, and you're rolling over. Never mind, you'll get there with a bit of practice. Come along now, let's go this way.'

The large kingfish flicked its tail fin and shot off down towards a stony archway in the coral. Micky tried to copy him. He flicked his tail fin and, still on his side, swam off in the opposite direction.

'I said this way,' shouted the kingfish and, with great difficulty, Micky tried to follow. He moved his left arm and shot up to the surface. He moved his right arm and shot down to the sand. He moved both together and found himself going round in circles. Finally, he gave up and floated upside down.

The kingfish swam into view and peered at him kindly. 'You know, it's really quite simple. Just do as I do. Now, feet together. Off we go.'

This time Micky shot straight into the coral and banged his nose.

'Oh dear,' Mr Brown sounded quite upset. 'Perhaps we were too adventurous on our first outing. Let's head back to the boat.'

The large kingfish slowly made its way up towards the surface while the smaller fish followed in a series of jerks and zigzags – rather like Morse code.

Dot – dot – dot. It jerked sideways.

Dash – dash – dash. It rushed up a few feet.

Finally, Micky's head broke the surface a little way from the boat. Mr Brown was already back on board. He spoke to

Hector and Lysander. They took off, landing in the water beside the exhausted boy, helping him the last few feet.

'Wow!' sighed Micky, safely seated once again in the boat. 'That was really something.'

The old man draped his seaweed shawl round the boy, to stop him catching cold, and disappeared into the cabin. He returned a few minutes later with a glass full of something greenish-white.

'Here,' he handed Micky the glass. 'I think you need something to drink.'

Micky obediently drank. 'Golly, that's good, I don't feel tired at all now. What is it?'

'We call it seamoss. It's made from seaweed.'

'Seaweed! Yuck!' exclaimed Micky unable to stop himself. Then, he added a bit shamefaced, 'But it's smashing, just like a milkshake.'

The old man laughed. 'It's better for you than even a milkshake. Would you like another?'

Micky nodded. Mr Brown got up again and, taking Micky's glass, disappeared once more.

Micky put on his glasses and peered down through the clear water towards the reef, as the boat chugged quietly towards the shore. Was he dreaming? He pinched himself. Ouch! He was awake all right. He stared down at his arms and legs. Nothing different about them at all. So? He made himself ask the question that had been bothering him ever since he got back in the boat. Had he really been changed into a fish? Cautiously his fingers crept up to his nose and rubbed it. There really WAS a graze there AND it hurt.

He looked up as the old man came back on deck again, carrying two glasses of seamoss.

'Was I …' he began.

'Oh yes,' said Mr Brown, handing Micky his seamoss milkshake. 'You told me your brother could swim like a fish. I thought the best way for you to do the same is to become a fish – simple really.'

His bright eyes twinkled at Micky. Then, taking a sip of his seamoss, he picked up a small fish from a plastic bucket and offered it to Hector, who gulped it down. Immediately Lysander flew off to find one for himself.

Micky's mouth opened and stayed open. *He hadn't said anything about his brother swimming.*

The boat ran back up the sand, exactly as if it had legs, and stopped. Mr Brown, turning round, caught Micky's look of amazement and laughed.

'I'm far too old to be hauling boats about. Now, hurry up and finish your drink or you'll miss your bus. Come back tomorrow and we'll have another go. I'll be waiting for you.'

Before Micky could think of anything to say, he was back on shore waiting for the bus. It roared into view round the long bend and screeched to a halt. Micky scrambled on paying his fare to the conductor, who sat up front. He turned to wave. '*Come on, bus, hurry up,*' he said quietly to himself. '*I'm going swimming again tomorrow.*'

'And Micky's not a bit of trouble now, dear,' said Mrs Wells. 'He does his homework without being told and eats everything I put in front of him. All he wants to do is rush off with old Mr Brown for his swimming lessons.'

'Mmm, that's nice, dear,' said Mr Wells not listening to a word his wife said.

Mrs Wells sighed. 'And Penny's gone off boys, thank goodness. She spends all her time with her girlfriends now. She's even being nice to Micky.'

'Yes, that's right, dear,' said Mr Wells, not looking up from his papers.

Mrs Wells tried again. 'And our next door neighbour's got some pigs, which flew right round the island last night and he had a terrible time catching them.'

Mr Wells heard that. 'Pigs, our neighbour's got pigs! Really, dear, I've never heard such nonsense. Well, I've got to go, I'm late.' He got up, hastily stuffing his papers into his briefcase.

'And what's Micky up to these days?' he said, on his way out of the door. 'Still giving you trouble? Never mind, I'll have a word with him tonight. Must go – bye.' Absentmindedly, giving Mrs Wells a kiss somewhere on her ear, he fled out to the car.

'Oh dear,' sighed Mrs Wells and went to do the washing up. 'Oh dear.'

A Day in School

Life was great and Micky was having such fun, he forgot all about trying to be difficult. Every afternoon, as soon as he'd done his homework, he grabbed his towel and shorts and rushed off to catch the bus to Oistins, the fishing village where he had met Mr Brown. At first, Mrs Wells insisted on going with him but she soon realised that in Barbados children could travel everywhere alone. It was such a small island, everyone knew everyone.

'I seed your boy learning to swim, mistress,' said the old lady, from whom she bought her oranges and bananas.

'That your boy I see on di beach?' called the green-coconut seller. 'My brudder, he got a boat too. He say de boy's doing well, better dan him, 'cos he never learned to swim nohow,' and went off chuckling.

So Micky, feeling very grown up,

40

caught the same bus every day, clutching his twenty-five cents for the fare. Soon the driver knew him and the conductor knew him and, even when there wasn't any room, everyone squeezed up a bit to let Micky climb aboard. Nobody minded, cheerfully chatting away, however much they were squashed.

Just like sunshine, thought Micky, as the bus thundered its way down the hot, dusty road, hooting and honking at anything that moved.

After the noise of the bus, Mr Brown's boat seemed peaceful and quiet. And, week after week, when the sea was blue and calm with little white frills on it, Micky put on the fins and jumped overboard. Of course, he knew if he said one single word at home about being a fish, not only would his parents *not* believe him but they'd *stop* him coming to the beach. So he kept quiet and enjoyed his lessons in the lovely blue sea.

Soon he could swim in a straight line, go round in a circle and up and down.

He didn't bang his nose on the coral now and he could dart in zigzags – *but he really wasn't much good at that.*

One day, when he was practising dives, he heard a splash close by, and the waves rocked him violently up and down. He looked up startled, to see the black shape of Lysander streak through the water, chasing his dinner. He caught the fish in his beak, swam up to the surface, and flew back to the boat. Micky watched the bird quickly swallow the fish, before diving back into the water to search for another. Micky found this rather worrying and climbed quickly back into the boat.

'Mr Brown, sir,' he said sounding nervous. 'May I ask you something important?'

Mr Brown peered at him over his spectacles. 'Ask away.'

'Well ... er, when I'm a fish in the sea, is there any chance Lysander might mistake me for his dinner?'

'My goodness me!' exclaimed the old man, astonished.

'Squaa-wwk!' shouted Hector indignantly and choked on the fish he was eating. Lysander shook his feathers angrily and started chattering fiercely to the old man. He hopped up and down on the stern rail so furiously he missed his footing, and only just stopped himself plunging into the sea, by wildly flapping his wings. He caused such a commotion that Mr Brown found it difficult to get a word in.

'Lysander, be quiet,' he ordered in a stern voice, trying not to laugh. 'You can't blame the boy – he doesn't know any better.' He attempted to calm the two angry birds.

'Know what?' said Micky, taken aback by the row he'd caused. 'I'm ever so sorry I upset Lysander, sir,' he admitted bravely.

'*Yes, yes*! No need to worry about that, he'll get over it. But I think it's time you went to school.'

'But I *go* to school,' protested Micky.

'Not that sort of school,' said Mr Brown. 'Haven't you heard of schools of whales and herrings?'

Micky couldn't honestly say he had.

'Well, come along then, we'd better be off. I'm sure school has started and we don't want to be late. In you go.'

The two kingfish swam through the calm sea towards the reef. The big one swam quite majestically, which is easy when you're nearly two metres long. The smaller one, however, trying to keep alongside, added the occasional zigzag or horizontal flip as it lost concentration and forgot to move its tail fin.

'You know,' the large kingfish chatted, 'there are things to learn under the sea just as there are on land. My goodness, if a fish didn't go to school he'd be eaten up in no time.'

Micky glanced nervously behind him and zigzagged into a frond of seaweed.

'The seabed is like a town,' explained the kingfish. 'It has roads and houses so you can easily find your way around. For example, to find the school, cross the main road and take the third road down on the left. Come along, this way.'

The kingfish disappeared round a bend in the reef wall and Micky flipped his feet as hard as he could to catch up.

'This is the outer reef,' explained the kingfish, when Micky came alongside again. 'Beyond it is the deep sea where all the big fish live. Look up.'

Micky obediently lay on his back and gazed up at the sea washing over the brown rocks. The outer reef wall was wide and beyond it the sea thundered into the barrier, breaking into foam and spray. Nothing could pass over the top of it; certainly not boats or big fish. Below the surface, the reef became grey and white and pink. Its rocky walls were covered with limpets and sea anemones, while seaweed and ferns grew out of every crevice, swaying gracefully in the current. It was like swimming through a forest.

The rock was pitted with holes and Micky, full of curiosity, poked his head into one. He backed out hurriedly in a flurry of sand, chased by an angry-looking fish flapping its tail in Micky's face.

'You do not peep into a fish's home unless you are invited,' reprimanded Mr Brown. 'If a hole is not inhabited, there will be a sign outside saying ... DUCK!'

Micky was just looking round to see where the duck was, when he saw the kingfish dive headfirst into the sand. Then he was tossed one way and another as the sea around him boiled and frothed. The sand was churned-up, the water became dark, and Micky couldn't see a thing. He heard the sound of giggling. Then he was barged and shoved and pushed and knocked and elbowed.

When the water was calm again and he could see, Micky found himself tied up in a cobweb of weed, which stuck to his fins like glue. He called to the kingfish, still lying motionless on the seabed.

'Mr Brown, sir, I'm stuck. I can't get free. Can you get me out?'

The huge fish dug himself out of the sand. He swam to where Micky was suspended in the web and started to prise Micky's fins out. Every time he got one free another got stuck.

'I say, Mr Brown,' gasped Micky. 'Whatever was that? Was it a whirlwind?'

'No!' said the kingfish sternly, when at last he got Micky free. 'Silly herrings, that's all. They go about in a gang, thousands of them swimming together and not one of them ever looks where it's going. It's no wonder they get caught in a fisherman's net. And it's no good sending them to school. They're too silly to learn anything. Look both ways now, we're crossing the main road.'

Micky hadn't been watching where they were going, still trying to remove the last bits of sticky web from his fins. Now he floated motionless, his mouth gaping open.

It was like a fancy dress parade. The fish were swimming slowly in a clockwise direction, bowing to the kingfish who naturally bowed back. Every colour of the rainbow was represented, plus a few others that had never seen a rainbow. There was a greenish-bluish-purplish colour belonging to a flat fish with a huge fan on its head. And a greyish-whitish-salmonish colour, decorated all over with pink spots, which belonged to a fish with huge lips. Every time this fish breathed out, it blew out a swarm of tiny red fish. When it sucked in, the red fish disappeared inside its mouth again.

'Why are they bowing to you, sir?' asked Micky.

'You see in the jungle the lion is king. Now, under the sea, the kingfish is rather like that. He doesn't have any natural enemies. After all, look at my size. Now remember,' Mr Brown called, as they crossed the main road. 'Three roads down on the left.'

Micky found himself in a rocky clearing, In front of him was an archway and, hanging from it, a big board with the words: *School Only*.

'Here we are,' said the kingfish and swam through the archway, leaving Micky to follow.

His entrance into the school, all one hundred and eighty-five centimetres of him, caused an uproar. Half the baby fish had never seen anything so big. Remembering what their mothers said: *If it's big it's bound to be dangerous*, they dived headfirst into the sand and lay there, with only their tails sticking out. The rest tried to get behind a large mackerel, who was busily writing on a blackboard.

The mackerel beamed when he saw them and, taking no notice of the commotion, swam over.

'Aye, good morning, Mr Brown, sir. What a privilege to have you in my school. But, if you don't mind, we'd better talk outside.'

He turned round, addressing the huddle of fishes.

'As you've behaved so rudely to our visitors, you'd

better practise the first lesson,' he said sternly. He picked up a small crab from the sand and placed it on a round rock at the front of the classroom. 'I'll be back in two minutes.' Then, leading the way, he swam back through the arch followed by Micky and Mr Brown.

'So you're the wee laddie we've been hearing about.' The mackerel beamed at Micky.

It was a very weird thing, but Micky felt as if it was the first day at a new school and he was being interviewed by the headmaster. Even his tummy startled to jiggle about, as if it had butterflies in it. And what is more, he didn't think it the least bit peculiar to find a mackerel wearing glasses and speaking in a Scottish accent. (He knew it was a Scottish accent because his teacher at school came from Scotland.)

'Yes, sir,' he quavered nervously and would have raised his cap, if he had been wearing one.

'Aye, good manners I see, makes all the difference.' The mackerel nodded at Mr Brown. 'Young fish today don't have manners. Just look at those silly herring,' he added. 'So you want the laddie to spend the day with me. Aye, that's fine. He'll be just fine and you can collect him after school.'

'Sir, *you aren't going*?' gasped Micky in panic.

'Don't worry, lad, you'll be quite safe with Mr Mac here.

Nothing's going to happen to you inside the reef.'

'But, sir ...' began Micky. He stopped and gazed down at the sand in astonishment.

Coming into the clearing was a most amazing sight. It looked a bit like a fish. At least the rear end did, for Micky could see its tail jerking up and down. And the fish ...

... if it was a fish

... was jumping along the sand, sometimes banging into walls and sometimes standing on its head

... if it was its head.

The head ...

... if that's what it was

... was round and white.

Micky couldn't see any eyes, only smooth sides.

'Tut-tut!' said the kingfish. Stooping down, he used the tip of his fins to prise a yoghurt carton off the fish's head.

When he saw who had rescued him, the mullet blushed his thanks and rushed into school to tell his mates.

'Some of these youngsters never learn,' said the large kingfish sternly. 'Now go along, Micky, I'll be back when school closes. I know you'll have a most interesting day.'

'All right, sir,' gulped Micky bravely. 'But don't be late, will you?'

With a reassuring smile, the kingfish finned off down the road leading back to the boat.

'Come along, laddie, I must get on with my class. Two minutes will be there by now,' said the mackerel.

Lobster Pots

The rocky clearing was empty. Nothing stirred.

'Oh, I'm so sorry, sir, Mr Brown's scared them all away,' Micky exclaimed.

'Lordy bless us,' the mackeral laughed. 'But they're all still here.' He beamed.

'Very good, class. Now back in your places before Two Minutes.'

As he spoke he picked up the small crab, which had made its way across the stone, and placed it back in the centre.

'Mr Mac, sir, why do you keep picking up that crab?'

'That's Two Minutes, laddie. We don't have a school clock, so I use Two Minutes instead. It takes him exactly two minutes to get from the centre of this rock to the edge,' he explained. 'Watch!'

The little crab had been sidling as fast as it could towards the edge of the stone.

Mr Mac picked it up, putting it carefully back in the middle.

'As I said, two minutes, class.'

The sand swirled. Everywhere shapes pushed and shoved as fish fluttered and barged their way to their places. Micky blinked in surprise. As the water settled, he could see row upon row of fish, hovering motionless on the sand – the smallest in front, the largest behind. Mr Mac picked up the crab, which had nearly reached the edge of the rock, and put it down on the sand, where it immediately dug a hole and disappeared.

'You beat Two Minutes,' he said. 'Excellent! That, laddie, is the first rule of the sea.'

'What is that, sir?'

'*Camouflage*. If something big comes along looking for a meal – hide. Mullet B, what is the next rule?'

A young mullet, in the row next to Micky, swam to the front of the class. Micky recognised it as the one they had rescued from the yoghurt pot.

'Never go out alone and stay inside the reef.'

'Well done, laddie,' Mr Mac patted him on the head. The mullet blushed and finned back to his place.

'Now, lassies and laddies, we will do *Know your Fish*. Which fish is the most dangerous?' he said to Micky.

'The shark, I think.'

The class tittered.

'Not a bad guess, laddie.' Mr Mac beamed at him. 'But not quite right. Now you, laddie ...' He pointed to a red mullet that spent all its time opening and closing its mouth.

'The whale, sir,' it squeaked.

The class tittered even more. The red mullet went quite white with embarrassment and hid in the sand, with only its tail showing.

'Doesn't anyone know?' asked Mr Mac sternly, waving his glasses.

'Yes, sir, me, sir.' A brown flat-nosed fish spoke up. 'It's the barracuda, sir.'

'Right, laddie, and has anyone ever seen a barracuda?'

The class of young fish shook their heads.

'Well, it has a wicked pointed jaw and vicious eyes and eats anything that moves, just for the fun of it. It can grow up to about ten fish-feet and has grey zigzag markings.

'Now this young man,' he pointed at Micky. 'He's a young kingfish. Note his markings, gold-brown swirls and splotches. He's a noble fish. Usually, of course, he lives beyond the reef but this young laddie is rather special.'

The entire class of fish stared at Micky. He blushed, wishing he could disappear into the sand like Two Minutes.

'Sir,' he said. 'What about birds?'

Micky had been dying to ask this question ever since he first entered the school but the moment he spoke, he wished he hadn't. The word BIRD obviously struck terror into the smaller fish. The sand bubbled and swirled. When Micky could see again, the first two rows of fish had disappeared.

Mr Mac took no notice of the strange behaviour of his pupils. 'Birds?' he said. 'Why birds?'

'Well, sir, could I be caught by a bird?'

'Why, laddie, I never heard such a thing. You must weigh a good ten pounds so a bird won't touch you. Fisherbirds,' he said lowering his voice to a whisper, 'Fisherbirds usually go for young herring or sardines that tramp around in shoals or NAUGHTY YOUNG FISH THAT DON'T PAY ATTENTION IN CLASS.'

Immediately, the sand bubbled up again as the fish dug themselves out and got back into their lines.

'Now recite your catechism. Herring G begin.'

Mr Mac pointed to the blackboard, so Herring G would know where to start, when another interruption took place. Into the classroom sidled a lobster. It hustled over to Mr Mac speaking in a high-pitched squeak. Micky understood only one word – *Albert*.

Mr Mac wasted no time. He picked up his cane, put on his spectacles, and calling, 'Laddie, come with me,' and 'Class, do your sums,' swam off through the archway, leaving Micky to follow.

Micky hadn't known that lobsters could swim fast but this one fairly whizzed along. Poor Micky had to beat his feet faster than he'd ever done before, to try and keep up. They swam down the main road, the strolling fish politely making way, and burst out of the rock into a sandy clearing. An extraordinary sight met their eyes. In the middle of the clearing was a lobster pot and, inside, was a lobster. Surrounding the pot, wringing their claws and dancing up and down on the sand, was its family – a mother lobster with five brothers and sisters.

'What's happened, Mr Mac, sir?' panted Micky, still out of breath.

'It's Albert. Every time they drop a lobster pot in this clearing, he gets himself into it and can't get out.'

Mother Lobster sidled up to him and started squeaking in the same silly way as the lobster that had brought them to the clearing. Micky couldn't understand her either.

'Aye, Mrs Lobster,' said Mr Mac soothingly. 'But I've tried speaking to the laddie. No, he takes no notice of me either. Aye, I know it's the fourth time this week. Well, if you want my advice you should leave him and let the fishermen haul him up. Aye, I know it's being cruel to be kind but it might teach him a lesson.'

He swam over to the pot and peered in.

'Albert,' he said in a stern voice. 'Next time you get in the pot, I've told your mother to leave you there and then we shall see.'

Albert's mother was still squeaking but at this Albert *and* his brothers and sisters joined in. What a noise!

Mr Mac took no further notice of them. He pushed one end of his cane between the bars of the pot, waving away the tiny tiddlers that were playing *dare* in and out of the bars.

'Can you lean on this end, laddie?' he said.

Micky pushed against the cane to open the bars. As soon as the opening was big enough, Albert sidled out. His mother, his brothers, and his sisters immediately fell on him and dragged him away, everyone squeaking loudly as they disappeared under the nearby rocks.

'You didn't really mean it, sir?' said Micky, as he and the mackerel swam leisurely back to the school. 'Did you?'

'Aye, I did.' The mackerel beamed at Micky. 'But don't worry, laddie, they'll soon throw him back, he's too small. But I won't be telling him that!'

iving on  the Wreck

It was Sunday morning. Mrs Wells gazed fondly at her family, all eating breakfast together. During the week, Mr Wells rushed off to work early followed by David, who refused point-blank to walk with his sister and brother to school. Today, Mr Wells had his head in an engineering journal, Micky was reading a book about tropical fish, and Penny and David were chatting about a beach party.

Then David ruined everything and shattered the peace of their family breakfast.

'Mum,' he said, 'Brian and I are going out with two instructors from the club – Julian and Peter. They are going to teach us to dive. Is that okay?'

'Wow! Can I go, too? *Can* I?' said Micky, longing to be included in one of his brother's outings.

'Stupid, you're too little.'

'No I'm not. I'm nearly nine now AND I can swim.'

'Yeah, I bet. With arm bands and doggy paddle.'

'No! I can swim properly. Oh do let me come?' pleaded Micky.

'You're *so* selfish, David,' said Penny in her best snooty voice. 'You never take him anywhere. You could at least let him go along and watch.'

'*You can talk*. I don't see *you* taking Micky with you when you go out with your friends,' shouted David, and the battle began in earnest.

'QUIET!' stormed Mr Wells. 'Is it too much to hope I can have some peace and quiet at the weekend?' He gathered up his papers. 'I*'m* going to work. At least it's peaceful there!'

'And I*'m* going diving.'

David leapt through the door, slamming it shut behind him. Penny began to cry and Micky buried his red face in his dish of cornflakes. *It wasn't fair. David still treated him like a baby and he wasn't. He knew much more about fish than David.*

'Oh dear,' sighed Mrs Wells gazing at the wreckage of her family. 'Oh dear.' And went to comfort Penny.

So Micky caught the bus and went off to see Mr Brown. He was always there, waiting across the road from the bus stop, just as if Mrs Wells had phoned him. He was such a comforting sight too, never cross or moody, and he didn't treat Micky like a baby.

'David upset you again, did he?'

Micky looked up quickly and grinned in spite of himself. *It was so weird how Mr Brown always knew what had happened.* 'Still, I do wish David could be my friend. I wish that more than anything in the world'.

'Hmm, do you now. Mmm? Well, let's see. I wonder if it could be arranged. Mmm, I think so.'

Micky let Mr Brown's mutterings wash over him, so used to his mother talking to herself. He busied himself stroking Hector and Lysander who, as usual, were perched on the rail.

'Well, if you feel brave enough,' continued Mr Brown, 'you can do a solo dive today while I stay in the boat. Yes, that's what we'll do. Come along now, in you go.'

Mr Brown took the wheel and the boat slid into the water. Try as he might, Micky couldn't see how it was done.

'It really is magic, sir, isn't it?'

Mr Brown's eyes twinkled. 'It's a beautiful day,' he said. 'Look, you can see your brother and his friends on their boat. 'Look – over there outside the reef.'

Micky shaded his eyes to see better in the bright sun. He sighed enviously. An idea suddenly struck him. 'Sir, could I swim over and see what they're doing? I mean, I wouldn't go outside the reef or anything.'

'That should be all right. You swim very well now and I believe you to be sensible enough to keep away from danger. Off you go then. Hector and Lysander will keep you company.'

Immediately the two birds flew off their perch on the stern rail and landed on the sea, chattering to each other as they paddled along waiting for Micky to put on the green fins.

Oh, *how marvellous*, thought Micky as he finned along all on his own. *I've got the whole ocean to play in.* In his excitement he did two flips, a somersault, and a twist, facing the reef again.

The water was cool and clear and as soft as silk, the nicest feeling Micky could ever remember. He waved to a passing bass who waved back, and skimmed on, loving ever second.

The divers' boat had anchored way out beyond the reef and the group of boys had swum in. They were intending to explore an old wreck, which lay in about fifty feet of water just inside the reef wall. Micky could see them quite clearly, with their air-tanks and fins, as they swam down towards the seabed.

Many years before, the wreck had been a cargo boat, sailing between the islands. During a gale, it had struck the reef and sunk. Now, it was home to thousands of fish and corals, crabs and eels. Groups of divers were constantly exploring it, but the fish were so used to them they took no notice, simply going on about their business.

If only David knew I was here, thought Micky, keeping in the shadow of the reef. The instructors were carrying spear guns and, although there was a law banning spear-fishing inside the reef, Micky didn't want to risk being shot at.

Eventually, the group of boys gathered up their trophies of shells and coral, putting them in bags which they carried round their waists. One by one, they began to swim towards the top of the reef wall. Brian, who was lagging behind, pointed at something on the sand and, unnoticed by the rest of the group, swam down again to have a look. The other divers continued towards the boat. Soon, all Micky could see of them was five pairs of fins and some bubbles.

Brian made his way along the sea bed, poking in and out of the crevices in the rocks. He picked up a Coke bottle and threw it down again, while Micky stayed close, practising Mr Mac's lesson in camouflage. Slowly, Brian moved towards a part of the reef that Micky had never visited before. Here, the reef wall was broken in places. Brian climbed over the rocks and, next moment, he had dived off the other side and disappeared from view on the seabed beyond.

Micky didn't know what to do. Someone had to get Brian back inside the reef wall. Didn't he know how dangerous it was on his own outside the reef? Besides, his friends didn't know where he was. He would have to swim to the boat and tell them.

Micky stared doubtfully at the cloudy ocean, which had swallowed Brian up. It was far too scary to go that way. He swam swiftly back along the coral searching for a gap. Using the reef wall as cover, he could leave crossing the deep open water until the very last moment. *There*! In front of him appeared a crack wide enough for him to swim through. A moment later and he was on the outside, facing the big ocean.

The space in front of him was vast and empty, nothing but greyish sand with a few sand-coloured rocks and sand-coloured weed. It was dim and dark, the water shadowy and murky. Micky shivered. It was much colder here too.

Hurrah! Brian was still there, poking among the rocks on the seabed. Micky glanced up towards the surface, a long way above them. There was no sign of the boat but it had to be there, somewhere beyond this vast empty space.

Oh thank goodness! Micky sighed happily as he spotted the dark shape in the distance. The instructors had at last realised Brian was missing and had sent someone to look for him. Micky headed quickly back towards the gap in the reef wall. He hated out there, it was really scary. He reached the rock but the scared feeling refused to go away. It felt creepy, as if something dreadful was about to happen.

I bet Brian will get a wigging from the instructor for not obeying the rules, he thought. He peeped round the rock to see if he could still see Brian, and STARED STRAIGHT INTO THE FACE OF THE BIGGEST FISH HE HAD EVER SEEN!

olonel red

Micky was terrified. He hovered, unable to move, staring at the monstrous fish coming closer and closer. He had to do something but what? He'd ask Mr Mac, he'd know.

Pulling back into the crack out of sight Micky, silently but with great speed, flicked his fins and swam back along the coral pathway in the direction of the school. His luck was in. There was his teacher friend writing on the blackboard and whistling a ditty, just as if he had never heard the word shark.

'Mr Mackerel, Mac, sir!' Poor Micky could hardly speak he was so out of breath.

'Well now, laddie and what's your hurry?'

Mac peered through his spectacles at the gasping kingfish. He pushed them back on to his forehead in order to see him more clearly.

'*Shark*!' My friend's being attacked by a shark,' Micky panted.

'You're not serious,' Mr Mac looked shocked. 'Well, laddie, I'm right sorry for your friend but there's nothing you can do. It's the law of nature, big eats little.'

'Oh no, sir, you've got it all wrong.' Micky tried to steady his breathing. 'It's a *human* friend and I've simply got to find a way to rescue him.'

'A human! *And what's more a friend of yours*. That makes a difference.' Mac shook his head, pushing his glasses back on to his nose. 'I think we'd better have a spot of help with this.'

He picked up the conch shell that was hanging on the wall and blew a tremendous blast to summon the school.

Immediately dozens of fish appeared: little fish and tiny fish – plain fish and coloured fish – striped fish and spotted fish – long fish and short fish – flat fish and round fish. All of them graduates of the school. So many ripples were caused by the fish, jostling for a good view of Micky, that the mackerel had to wave his spectacles at them, to quieten them down.

'Now, laddies, we've not got time for chattering, nice though it may be. I think most of you have met our kingfish friend here,' he said, waving his spectacles in Micky's direction. 'Well now, his human friend is under attack from a shark and ...'

Such a twittering came from the crowd of fish that he couldn't continue. At the mention of the word *shark* some of the fish went pale at the gills. One red snapper actually fainted and became quite white, while others turned upside down, to make sure the shark wasn't about to jump on them. Indeed, the blowfish blew himself up out of sheer nervousness and the conch disappeared into his shell.

Mr Mac was furious. He jumped up and down, waving his glasses for silence. 'You're a daft lot of fish. Stop behaving like a school of herrings. You know *perfectly well* a shark *can't get inside the reef*!'

Mac's words were greeted with audible relief, although the blowfish only half-deflated himself, just in case; while the conch thought he could hear what Mac was saying – quite well enough, thank you, with only one horn outside his shell.

'As I was saying,' Mac continued when it was quiet. 'A shark is menacing this laddie's friend on the *outer* reef. The question is what do we do to save him?'

At the mention of the word Shark

Silence!

'Please.' It was Micky who spoke. 'Please, we have to do something. He's not very old and his friends in the boat don't know where he is, so they can't help.'

'Well then, laddie, I think we'd better all go and try to rescue this boy ourselves.' Full of enthusiasm, his Scottish fighting blood beginning to stir, Mr Mac was ready for anything. But, for the other fish, the idea was quite monstrous. After all, a shark could swallow them all in one mouthful – or anyway in two. The young red snapper fainted away again and some of the others discovered they were late for appointments and vanished.

'Excuse me, sir,' a young mackerel, class of '99, spoke up. 'Could Matilda help?'

'What an extraordinary idea! Aye, but if you think about it, it's the perfect answer. Why ever didn't I think of Matilda.' Mac beamed all round.

'Who's Matilda?' said Micky curiously.

'You've not met Matilda yet?'

Micky shook his head.

'Well, laddie, you have a real pleasure to come. A real lady is Matilda. She's a whale, you know, and usually around here at this time of the year.'

The young mackerel spoke again. 'Sir, I saw her this morning. She said she was heading north to visit the islands.'

'Well, bless me,' Mac sounded mildly concerned. 'Isn't that just like a woman to go off on a jaunt when you need her?' He called out, 'Is François here, the leader of the flying fish?'

A handsome dark navy fish, his fins long and powerful, swam out of the crowd.

'Well, now, it's a good thing you haven't gone off on a jaunt. Get your lads together and fly up to St. Vincent, there's a good laddie. Find Matilda and get her back here as quickly as possible.'

The Flying Fish bowed elegantly and, with a graceful flourish, vanished through the coral.

'But that might take hours if Matilda has gone north,' Micky pointed out.

'Now don't you worry your wee head, laddie, François will find her and bring her back in plenty of time.'

Mac picked up his chalk and turned back to the blackboard. The remaining fish began to swim off, anxious to get home before they got involved in shark fighting.

'But, sir, my friend only has air for about half an hour,' Micky persisted.

'*Confound it!*' Mac swore. 'I beg your pardon, laddie, but I quite forgot humans need air. Now we are in a pickle. Whatever can we do?'

A squeaky voice rose up to them out of the sand. 'Ask the colonel, he'll help.'

They looked down to see a young squib waving his arms about in his effort to attract their attention.

'The colonel's fought sharks before *and* won,' he added proudly.

'Bless my soul. Is Colonel Fred still fighting sharks? Well done, young Fred. We'll go and consult the colonel. Come along now, we must hurry.'

The mackerel swam off through the coral leaving Micky and young Fred to follow as best they could. Young Fred swooped along quite happily in his jerky fashion, talking non-stop about how wonderful Uncle Fred was and didn't even bother to look where they were going. Poor Micky, it was all he could do to keep the mackerel's tail fin in view. He didn't even have breath enough to listen.

He was just in time to see his teacher friend disappear through a narrow arch in the centre of huge barrier of rock. Micky quickly followed, the tunnel twisting and turning. It rose sharply upwards and Micky was blinded by brilliant light. When he could see again, he found himself in a rocky chamber, into which were pouring shafts of gold sunlight. Its walls were decorated with long strands of seaweed and beautiful ferns. Fast asleep, on a flat rock in the middle of a pool of sunlight, was a large octopus. To Micky's astonishment, the octopus sported a military moustache while, lying by his side, was an army cap bearing the insignia of a full colonel *and* a swagger stick.

'Fred, Colonel, wake-up there's a good fellow. I say, Colonel.' Mac swam round and round the octopus trying to waken him.

The octopus opened his eyes and sat up, instantly alert. 'What brings you here, Mac? Rioting in your school? War broken out, eh?'

'Thank goodness you're awake, Fred. No, you know quite well I don't have trouble in my school. It's far worse than that. We've got a shark!'

'Shark, eh? *That is good news*. It's been pretty dull round here recently, you know.' The octopus twirled his moustache, put on his cap and picked up his cane – all at the same time. 'Who's this? This, the young kingfish you were telling me about, the one that's really a boy?'

'Yes, Fred, of course it is. As if there would be two such kingfish.' Poor Mr Mac did sound agitated. He beckoned Micky. 'May I present Colonel Fred, the Commander of the Army.'

The colonel nodded. 'Right lad. Speak up. What's the problem?'

'Well, sir, it's my friend. He's caught behind some rocks beyond the reef and there's a shark trying to kill him. Mr Mac has sent for Matilda but she may not get here in time. Your nephew suggested you might help.'

'Quite right, too. Good thinking, young Fred.'

One of the colonel's large tentacles patted young Fred absentmindedly on the head. Young Fred blushed.

'Right then,' ordered the colonel. 'No time for hanging around. Action's the word.'

He whistled loudly through one of his tentacles.

… not the one that was twirling his moustache

…nor the one putting on his cap

…nor the one patting young Fred on the head

…another one.

At the same time, tucking his cane under an arm he shot off along the dark tunnel towards the entrance to the rocky barrier, leaving the others to follow as best they could.

Now what's going to happen, thought Micky excitedly. *Now what?*

The Octopus Army

The clearing in front of the rocks was empty, nothing moved. The colonel whistled loudly again. As he did, the water around them grew legs – hundreds of legs. The coral was alive with octopus, quickly and silently moving towards them.

The colonel barked, '*Atten – shun*! *Form ranks* ON the double.'

Micky's mouth gaped open. He couldn't believe what he was seeing. One moment the water was thrashing about, as dozens of octopus surged here and there, then everything was still. Now, before him, appeared rank upon rank of soldiers, perfectly at attention. Their bodies to the front, their tentacles arranged in strict order behind.

'Sergeant,' bellowed the colonel.

'SIR!' A huge octopus stepped out of line and saluted.

'Number them off.'

'Very good, SIR.'

The sergeant, in a stentorian voice, started to take the roll-call.

'Kingfish?' Colonel Fred beckoned Micky forward. 'Can you lead us to the shark?'

Poor Micky, he still hadn't recovered from the shock of seeing the octopus army. He shook his head trying to collect his scattered wits. There was something rather special about this colonel.

'I think so, sir. He's on the outer reef near where the old fishing boat sunk.'

'Right then! Now, lad, during this exercise you will hold the honorary rank of lieutenant.'

Micky nodded, absolutely thrilled.

The colonel turned to the hovering school teacher.

'Mac, old friend. Can't take you along on this little caper. You're a teacher not a soldier. We need your help to evacuate the fish from the battle zone. Can't have civilians getting caught up in a war, don't you know.'

Mac nodded. 'Aye, you're right. See you tomorrow, laddie, and good luck.'

With a flick of his fins, he swam off in the direction of the school to sound the alarm.

'Colonel, SIR.' The sergeant saluted. 'Privates Washington and Wellington are absent on the outer reef and Corporal Rommel is sick, SIR.'

'Thank you, Sergeant,' nodded the colonel. 'Right, squadron. Stand at ease. All you need to know is that *this is the big one*. You've been trained for this, lads. So let's go get him. Right! Sergeant, take us out.'

'SQUADRR – ONN on my mark … QUU – ick march. Out in – Out in – Out in – Out in.'

With Micky leading, out marched the squadron of octopus.

On the count of *out* – out shot their heads; their legs *all eight of them* straight out behind their bodies.

On the count of *in* – their legs bent up smartly, like a frog's legs do when they're swimming.

Out in – out in – out in – out in …

Back along the inner reef they marched, along the route that Micky had raced a short while before. As they marched in total silence, they passed fish hastily swimming away from the reef and the battle zone.

'We're there,' Micky whispered.

'SQUADRR – ONN HALT!'

The command was given with such abruptness, that the smaller octopus in the rear shot head first into the chap in front. There was much sorting out of legs before the lines were straight again.

'Corporals Nelson and Napoleon,' ordered the colonel. 'Step forward.'

'SIR!' Two large octopus, nearly as large as the colonel, saluted and moved out of the ranks.

'Right, lads, you know what to do. Exact lay-out of the ground. Assessment of the current situation. And be quick about it. No noise and don't take chances.'

The corporals saluted, turned and slithered silently up the coral and were soon lost to view.

hundreds of legs

They had reached an open sandy area on the inside of the reef. Immediately in front of Micky was the narrow gap through which he had swum, and, somewhere on the outer side of the reef, the shark. The colonel moved into the gap and peered through it. Micky finned quietly to his side. There was nothing to be seen. The place where the shark had been was empty!

They were too late!

The colonel patted Micky on the shoulder. 'Now lad, there's not a bit of good speculating what's happened.' He seemed to be able to read Micky's thoughts. 'Just wait patiently till the scouts report in. Sergeant? Let the men stand at ease,' he instructed quietly.

They waited. Micky impatiently swimming round and round the clearing; the colonel nonchalantly swinging his cane, twirling his moustache, and gazing at nothing in particular, as if he had never heard the word shark. The army standing at ease on the sand, rank upon rank of dark black bodies, here and there dotted with a pale brown one.

There came a slight rustle of ferns from the coral above. The two corporals slid quietly down the reef halting in front of the colonel.

'Scouts reporting in, sir.' It was Corporal Nelson.

'Come on, lad, be quick about it.'

'He's there all right, sir.'

Micky sighed thankfully.

'The human is backed right up against the reef wall. The shark is attacking but it can't get at him.'

'By the way, sir,' Corporal Nelson added. 'It's that nasty

brute we tangled with a while back, the one with the hook in its jaw.'

The Colonel nodded. 'Old Hookjaw, eh. Did he spot you?'

'Oh no, sir.' Corporal Nelson sounded shocked by the suggestion. 'But we've got to go in quickly. The human's in trouble, he's breathing very slowly.'

'That means he's coming to the end of his air and trying to make it last as long as possible,' cried Micky. 'Please hurry.'

'Patience, lad. We'll get him, don't fret. Sergeant?'

'SIR!' The huge octopus with enormous tentacles, larger even than the colonel's (he was their champion wrestler), swam forward and saluted.

'You're to lead the rescue party. Corporals Nelson and Napoleon will go with you and show you the way. The lieutenant will go also. Make sure nothing happens to him.'

The sergeant nodded. 'Yes, SIR.'

'Go in quickly over the coral, and keep well under cover. As soon as you hear the signal for attack, pull the human up the reef.' The colonel waved Micky forward. 'Lieutenant, keep close to the sergeant. Your job is to find the boat. If it's not there, the sergeant will take the diver into the inner reef and get him out of the water, while you go for help.'

Micky nodded.

'Right, then. Everything understood.'

The three octopus saluted.

'Off you go. Good luck.'

The Colonel addressed the squadron. 'Right, lads, we're off. We'll go in as soon as the sergeant's party is in position.

On my command, fire at will but move fast. As you clear the shark's path, get back in the coral and stay there. When the situation resolves itself, make your way back to this clearing and report in. Quietly now, lads, single file through the gap. Form up on the other side.'

The sergeant, Corporals Nelson and Napoleon, with Micky following closely behind, slithered quietly over the coral. Up the rocks they climbed to the top of the reef wall. Slowly they moved along the top of the barrier, towards the spot where the scouts had pinpointed the shark. Corporal Nelson stayed close to Micky, pointing out banks of fern behind which he could dart for cover.

Closer and closer they came. Now, in front of them, they could see the sand disturbed by the furious passing of the shark. Now, the water was swirling from the movement of its large and vicious body. Behind them, the colonel was crouching low in the sand waving his troops into position. Micky watched the octopus army slithering silently through the narrow gap, only to disappear from view on the sea bed.

Above him the water was clear and calm, reflecting no trace of the battle about to be fought. Micky stared about him trying to spot the anchor rope from the divers' boat.

Surely they wouldn't have left. Yes! There! Faintly, in the distance, Micky spotted the fine line of the anchor rope. *But it was an awful a long way to swim across open water if you're being hunted by a shark.*

He touched the sergeant's arm and pointed. The octopus nodded and continued on his silent way. They had arrived.

The two corporals, a little way ahead of them, gave a *thumbs-down* sign. Micky peered over the edge of the reef and gasped with shock.

There, directly beneath him, not two metres away, was the shark. Driving the whole of its huge length, with tremendous speed and anger, it surged towards the rock where Brian was crouched – pulling away at the last moment. Micky spotted the bubbles of air escaping from the diver's mask, almost lost in the turbulence caused by the shark's movement through the water.

Hurrah, they were in time!

The Rescue

The sergeant pulled Micky back behind some ferns, signalling him to stay put. The three soldiers lay flat on the rocky surface – exactly like lumps of coral. Completely invisible, except for their eyes glinting, they watched every movement of the shark. It swam away, swinging round again to make another run. Micky saw the great fin cutting the water, the teeth white and pointed in its open mouth, the fish hook lodged in its jaw. As the shark veered away from the rocks, Micky heard a whistle from the reef behind. The silvery-coloured monster swung round powering in again at full speed. The whistle sounded again.

Fire at Will!

The three octopus were down the coral in a flash, tentacles outstretched. They wrapped themselves firmly round the diver, pulling him away from the rocks. At the same time, a wall of black bodies passed in front of them, putting themselves between the rescue party and the path of the shark, already streaking in for another attack. Then Micky saw nothing. The sea in front of him was inky black.

No *octopus, no shark, nothing*! The army had attacked.

A voice whispered, 'Come along, lad, don't hang about. We've got to get to the boat before the shark realises his dinner has gone.'

Micky headed for open water, slanting upwards towards the distant outline of the anchor rope. The sergeant, by his side, held the diver, while the two corporals brought up the rear, trailing ink as a smoke screen. But the surface was approaching fast, *too fast*.

'Stop, stop!' shouted Micky. 'We've got to let the diver adjust to the new depth.'

The sergeant obediently stopped.

'How long have we got to stay here, Lieutenant?' he said. 'Bad position. No shelter here in open water.'

'I don't know,' confessed Micky, shaking with fright, his head constantly swivelling round to look behind him. 'I only know he's been down so long and so deep, he has to stop. If we take him up too fast, he'll get very sick. It's something to do with the type of air he carries on his back.'

'Corporal Nelson, get down below and check on the position of the shark. Try and reach the colonel and advise him of the situation. Whistle twice for danger,' ordered the sergeant quietly.

The corporal saluted, vanishing into the inky smoke-screen still trailing below them. They waited, the sergeant holding the motionless diver. His eyes searched the water from side to side while Micky counted off the vital seconds, praying he was doing the right thing. He could see the outline of the boat now quite clearly above him – so near and yet so far. He counted, begging for the seconds to pass quickly and for the shark to keep away.

Then he heard a whistle!

'*What do we do now*?' Micky quavered.

'Off you go to the boat as fast as you can and get a few humans down here,' the sergeant instructed, as calmly if they were in a paddling pool with a goldfish, not a hundred and fifty metres from safety in the open sea, with a man-eating shark chasing them.

'B-b-b-but what are you going to do?' stuttered Micky.

'Do, lad? Why stay right here and finish the job. Now off with you.'

The calm voice reassured him. Micky swam towards the boat as fast as he could, not daring to look behind him. His head broke the surface a short distance from the boat, to find his brother and the other divers peering anxiously over the side.

'Micky!' exclaimed his brother. 'Whatever are you doing here?'

'Have you seen Brian?' said Julian, one of the instructors. 'He's missing. We've been searching.'

'Brian's in trouble,' gasped Micky. 'He's coming up but he's below me and there's a shark about. I came for help.'

Willing hands pulled him over the side of the boat. Julian and Peter strapped on their tanks and masks. Then, grabbing their spear guns, dived straight into the water heading for the spot where Micky was pointing.

Micky took off his fins, dumping them onto the floor of the boat, while David wrapped a towel round him.

'Did you really see a shark, Micky, or were you imagining it?' David asked him in a low voice.

'Oh no,' Micky shook his head. Still worried, he leaned over the side trying to see into the water. 'There's a shark there all right. It had Brian pinned down for ages.'

Someone handed Micky a Coke but he ignored it. He ignored their eager questions too, his eyes fixed on the spot where the two instructors had gone down.

By this time all the boys were anxiously peering over the side. As they watched, the sea around the boat became cloudy. Then it became streaked with a dark black substance, as if someone had emptied a bottle of ink into it. They heard a splash as the divers surfaced, holding Brian between them. The little group of boys shouted with joy, eagerly pulling Brian from the sea.

'Look! Over there!' David pointed towards the dark black sea. The two instructors, still only halfway into the boat, swivelled round to stare at the dozens of black heads bobbing in a sea of ink. Micky raised his arm to salute one of them; the one to which a military moustache was attached. An eye winked and an arm flashed a thumbs-up sign. Then the head vanished and the sea became clear and empty again.

Micky felt like singing and dancing with joy. *They'd done it, they'd really done it. They had beaten the shark.*

The rest of the group were too busy clustering round Brian to take any notice of Micky. Draped in a blanket and sipping a drink, Brian was quickly recovering from his ordeal and trying to answer all the questions the boys threw at him.

'Micky, *Micky* for goodness sake, *stop daydreaming.*'

Micky came to with a start. 'What's that, David? What did you say?'

'Brian was asking if you pulled him off the rocks?' his brother said, relaying the question from Brian.

'What do you remember, Brian?' said Micky, stalling for time, in order to come up with some sort of answer.

'That's just the trouble, it was so dark. One minute I was happily looking for shells and the next ... there was *that shark.*' Brian shuddered. 'Oh! He was monstrous with a huge hook in his jaw. I got behind a rock but he was determined to get me. He was only inches away.' Brian shuddered again. 'I was getting to the end of my air too and I was just thinking I would have to make a run for it ... I know it was stupid. But I had no choice. Then it all went dark. I must have blacked out. Except I swear I felt someone pulling me up the reef. The strange thing is it felt like several people.'

The next question came.

'Did you dive down, Micky, and pull him off the rocks?'

Micky was silent. Whatever could he say? He'd been brought up to tell the truth but now if he did, everyone would think he was crazy.

'Er ... I was out swimming on my own,' he muttered, 'when I saw your boat and ... er ... I thought it would be nice to swim over and say hello.'

At *least that bit's true*, he thought. 'That's when I saw Brian down below and then I saw the shark. Brian seemed to be stuck behind a rock but it was very dark and I couldn't see much. I moved along the top of the reef to try and help and one minute he was behind the rock and the next he seemed to be free and ... er ... coming up with me. I swam on ahead to get help, in case the shark followed.'

'And there isn't anything more?' said Julian, looking at him suspiciously. 'What about the arms pulling Brian off the rock – were they yours?'

'I can't explain that,' said Micky honestly, shaking his head.

'And where is the shark?' said Peter, the assistant instructor. 'There was no sign of him when we got to you, Brian, only those octopuses.'

'Perhaps that's what you felt,' suggested David. 'Perhaps you got entangled with an octopus. If you blacked out it could have felt like arms.'

'Yes,' agreed Julian. 'That's most likely what happened.'

Micky couldn't stop himself grinning. *If only David knew how close he'd come to what really happened on the reef.*

'Well, I've never known anything like it in all my days of diving,' said Julian. '*You*, Brian, have had a very lucky escape. I've never known a shark leave a prey, unless something happens to scare it off. And *you*, young Micky, *well done*. You've really proved yourself today. You did something many a man would have hesitated to do. It took a lot of courage to stay and help Brian.'

He nodded at David.

'You should be *pretty proud* to have a youngster like that for a brother. *He's all right*.'

'I know,' said David. '*And I am!*'

Micky blushed. His brother was actually praising him, instead of calling him a miserable little worm. He sat up straight, feeling quite wonderful.

'As for you, Brian,' continued the instructor. 'You and I will have a little chat about the rules of diving when we get ashore, *is that clear?*'

'Yes,' said Brian miserably.

'Right, lads. Up anchor, I want to get these two ashore and to the doctor as soon as possible.'

'We're fine,' Brian and Micky chorused together.

'Look here, Brian, you were down pretty deep. If what you say is true and you blacked out … remember, you came up pretty fast …'

'No, he didn't,' Micky interrupted without thinking. 'We equalised at the regulation depth and while I swam to warn you, the sergeant stayed …' He trailed off, his hand flying to cover his mouth to stop the words from getting out.

Luckily, Julian was too busy steering to take much notice. 'Don't bother to argue, young Micky, you're going to be checked out for my satisfaction, okay?'

Micky nodded. It was much easier to see the doctor, than answer any more questions.

The boat moved forward as the anchor came up over the side and was stowed away. They set course for the island, the others still questioning Brian about the shark and trying to piece together what had happened.

'Look! Flying fish off the port bow,' Julian shouted.

The boys looked up, staring. Dozens of beautiful navy

fish flew gracefully past above the waves, their gauze-like
wings fully outstretched. Then a huge animal rose out of
the sea. Micky just caught sight of one bright friendly eye,
before it disappeared into a vast cloud of spray, its tail fin

slapping the water with an echo like thunder.

Mouths opened in amazement. 'Heavens above! A whale! Whatever next! *Shark – octopus – flying fish* and now a whale.'

'Hurrah!' shouted Micky, without thinking. 'They found Matilda. She came after all!'

The words were out before Micky realised what he'd just said! All eyes turned to stare at him. There really was something very fishy about all this.

'Micky,' his brother glanced down at him and cuffed him playfully. 'Sometimes I think you're suffering from heat stroke. You certainly do say the weirdest things. I do wish you could act more like a normal human being.'

Micky grinned. He felt happy and excited, all the frightening bits fading from his mind.

'It was a smashing adventure,' he sighed. Then suddenly feeling terribly sleepy, he leaned back against his brother's shoulder.

'Tired, Micky?'

'Mmm, a bit. I've never had to swim such a long way and so fast.'

'Weren't you frightened when you saw the shark?'

'Oh yes, horribly, especially when I saw it so close by, but I wouldn't have missed the battle for anything.'

'What battle?' said his brother.

But Micky had fallen asleep, worn out with the excitement of the afternoon. The questions would have to wait.

All's Well that

 ends Well

Well, of course, lots of questions were asked. Brian was kept at home for a week and couldn't go to the beach. His father thought he'd got off *very lightly*, and said so, for at least an hour or two on the Sunday morning!

Mrs Wells thought Micky was wonderful; Brian's parents thought Micky was wonderful; Brian thought Micky was wonderful; and Penny thought her brother *so wonderful*, she boasted about him to all her friends.

But Mr Wells didn't.

'What do you mean you were swimming *alone*?' said Mr Wells sternly.

'It was the first time, Dad,' Micky answered truthfully.

'And just when did you learn to swim, *have you been having lessons*?'

Micky nodded.

'He can swim, Dad, I saw him,' said David, sticking up for his brother.

'Why didn't you tell me he was having lessons?' Mr Wells grumbled to his wife. 'I just don't know,' he muttered crossly, 'no one in this family tells me anything.'

Mrs Wells gazed at her husband in disbelief. Then picking up his newspaper hit him on the head with it! Micky gasped with astonishment, while Mr Wells gazed at his wife as if she had come from the planet Mars and he had never seen her before.

'What did you want to do that for?' he said rubbing his head.

'I've been telling you for months about Micky and all you ever say is: *yes, dear!*' stormed Mrs Wells.

'You've been telling me what for months?'

'About how good Micky is now and how he loves his swimming. And about … everything,' she said and burst into tears.

Mr Wells put his arm round her.

'I'm sorry, love,' he apologised. 'I get so busy at work, I forget about my family. I know, let's go to the beach right now and watch Micky swim.'

Ten minutes later Micky was on the beach, gazing at the water lapping at his feet, so nervous his teeth were chattering. After all he'd never swum without his fins before and now his family were watching. And he hadn't even got Mr Brown there to help him. He glanced behind him. His mum and dad nodded and smiled.

Micky tried desperately to remember all his lessons but his mind had gone blank. Legs together – use your feet only – arms by your sides and stretch …

'Come on, Micky,' shouted David, diving headfirst into the waves. 'I'll race you to the raft.'

Before Micky had time to think, he found himself in the water racing after David. A few minutes later he pulled himself up on to the raft, with David panting in behind him.

'Wow, Micky,' David said, when he'd got his breath back. 'Wherever did you learn to swim like that? I'm not racing you any more. Tell you what, though, if you want to come snorkelling with Brian and me – you can. And I'll use my pocket money to buy you a mask and fins. I reckon you deserve them, anyway, for saving Brian's life.'

Micky beamed with pride. It didn't matter being the youngest or having to go to bed early or having to wear glasses. He was the best and his grown-up brother had said so. Together they stood up and, diving into the water, swam back to shore.

aying oodbye

'Here I am,' shouted Micky, leaping on to the sand before the bus had hardly stopped moving, swinging the green fins. 'And did you hear what happened?' he added. He fell into step with Mr Brown as they crossed the road to the beach. 'I'm ever so sorry I haven't been to see you for ages but it's been a bit busy.'

Mr Brown smiled and nodded. 'Quite an adventure I understand and at last David is your friend. In that case all's well that ends well. I'm so glad you came today because I'm just about to leave.'

'Leave!' gasped Micky stunned. 'But *you can't*! You can't go now.'

Mr Brown looked at Micky's red face.

'Have you forgotten you are going back to England on Thursday?' he reminded gently.

Micky stood stock-still on the sand his mind whirling. *How did Mr Brown know that? Mum had only told him the night before.* 'How...' he began, then changed his mind. It wasn't any good asking wizards, they never told you how they did things. 'So I can't come and see you again?' He swallowed hard.

'Well,' said the old man. 'I rather think you will have too much to do before you leave. And you will enjoy going to school in England with your brother.'

'But I love you and Hector and Lysander,' burst out Micky. 'And I *love* swimming. Oh, *why* are you going?'

'Well, Matilda called in on her way south. She's off to the Antarctic. She came to tell me there is a little girl in St. Vincent who is very unhappy. So I'm going up there to look for myself. I expect I shall teach her to swim.'

'I never did meet Matilda,' sighed Micky enviously.

'Oh, I rather think you'll meet her one day,' said Mr Brown cheerfully, climbing aboard his fishing boat.

Hector and Lysander were perched in their usual place on the stern rail and Micky, crossing the deck, put his arms round them.

'Goodbye,' he said. 'I shall miss you.' The birds nuzzled his ear. 'Thank you, Mr Brown. Thank you for teaching me to swim.' He remembered his manners just in time but it was very difficult, with tears forcing their way up his throat. 'Will I see you again?' He got out the words in a rush.

'Yes, of course you will,' comforted Mr Brown. 'Don't forget Hookjaw is still about, although I don't think he'll bother anyone for a while. Matilda was so angry she chased him right up to Jamaica.'

Micky laughed in spite of his tears.

'Now, you had better hurry home again because your father is coming home early from work to take you and David swimming.'

'How do you know ...?' began Micky and then laughed. *It wasn't any good, wizards were wizards.* 'Goodbye, sir. Thank you.' He jumped over the side of the boat. He heard the bus coming round the corner by the police station and started to run. 'Goodbye and thank you.'

He panted up to the bus stop and the bus screeched to a halt. He leapt on and turned to wave but the sandy patch where the boat usually stood was empty. Shielding his eyes against the glare, he stared out to sea. Far out was a fishing boat and, flying above it, he could just make out two birds – one black and one white.

A tear rolled down Micky's cheek. He hastily brushed it away. He *would* miss Mr Brown. He sniffed.

The lady sitting in the seat in front turned round, her big round face beaming down at him.

'Now, young man,' she ordered. 'You too big now to cry, see. How old you are?'

'I'm nine,' said Micky.

'My, yor nearly a growed man,' laughed the lady. 'What you cryin' for?'

'We're going back to England soon.'

'Ah ha! What day you goin'?' she asked.

'We're going on Thursday,' said Micky, wondering what that had to do with anything.

'Den on Thursday, I'll put all me plants in de garden.'

'Why?' said Micky curiously.

'When someone nice leave Barbados, it always rain,' chuckled the lady.

'Does it? Always?'

'Always,' insisted the lady. 'If you nice people. And den you see de rain and you know you have to come back real soon.'

'Yes,' said Micky. 'Yes, I will.'

THE END

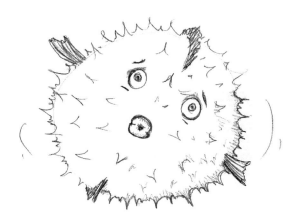